MW01005681

SUMMER

NANNY

A NOVELLA

AUDREY J.
COLE

RAINIER
PUBLISHING

ISBN: 9781098641153

CHAPTER ONE

"You should go," Bridgett said, pulling her lips away from her boyfriend's mouth.

Chris drew her closer. She pressed her hand against his chest. She inhaled and smelled the sweet scent of fresh cut grass mixed with sweat from working all day in the summer heat. As he wrapped his strong tan arms around her waist, she wished he could stay.

"I mean it. If Paul or Emily check the security camera and see your truck still parked in their driveway after dark, we'll both get fired."

Chris looked out the window at the darkening sky before turning back to Bridgett. The Fourth of July fireworks had already begun. Bridgett watched the explosions of color in the distance over Lake Washington.

"Five more minutes." He tucked Bridgett's straight blonde hair behind her shoulder and brought his mouth down to hers.

She slowly moved her palm down his chest as she allowed his tongue to re-enter her mouth. A cool breeze blew in through the open French doors that led to the expansive landscaped grounds of the Coopers' Seward Park waterfront mansion. She felt Chris's hand move down the side of her cutoff shorts. The back of the leather couch felt cold against her bare legs as Chris pressed her body against it.

It took nearly all her willpower to tear herself away from his arms. "It's dark out. You really have to go." She took her boyfriend's hand and led him out the French doors.

He didn't normally work on a holiday, but their employer, Emily, was hosting an extravagant gala tomorrow night at their home. She wanted the grounds to be perfect.

Bridgett looked into his brown eyes as they stood on the well-lit, second-story deck. "Paul and Emily were very clear when they hired me to watch Leo. No boyfriends over. Ever. And I can't afford to lose this job."

She'd been compensated more than generously by the retired actor and his much younger wife for watching their eighteen-month-old son for the summer. And she could use all the money she could get before starting dental school that fall at the University of Washington.

"I'll see you tomorrow," Bridgett said, letting go of his hand.

Chris leaned down and kissed her softly one last time, making her want to invite him back inside. She watched him walk to the end of the deck. He stopped at the top of the stairs that led to the backyard and turned to face her.

"Remember to turn the security alarm back on," he said before disappearing down the steps.

She smiled at his protectiveness and went inside. She locked the French door behind her. She moved through the English Tudor-style mansion to reset the alarm but stopped when she heard her phone chime atop the kitchen island.

She doubted it was Emily. Emily never bothered to

check on her child while Bridgett watched him. Paul, however, would sometimes call or text to check on his son.

She lifted her phone and saw it was a text from Chris. *Miss you already*. She grinned.

They'd met a month before, in early June. Chris had been doing landscape work on the rear of the property near where she'd taken Leo to play. She tried not to check him out while he worked, but she couldn't ignore the way his muscles bulged out of his t-shirt. He looked up and caught her stare and smiled. She couldn't help but smile back.

That night, they left the Coopers' at the same time. He stopped her as she was getting into her car and asked her out. They'd spent practically every spare moment together since. So far, their relationship had been everything a summer fling ought to be. If not more.

She started to text a reply when she heard a noise coming from upstairs—a noise that couldn't have come from a sleeping baby. It sounded like a door closing. Her fingers stilled and she looked toward the ceiling. But that couldn't have been what she'd heard. Other than sleeping Leo, she was alone in the house.

She jumped as her phone's cheerful ringtone filled the silent kitchen. Seeing the name on the caller ID, she exhaled. *Dad.* She lifted the phone to her ear.

"Hi, Dad."

"Hi, sweetheart. Sorry I missed your call earlier. My phone's been going in and out of service on the cruise. We just docked in Ketchikan, so I should have service until we leave tomorrow."

Bridgett returned her gaze to the ceiling. She hadn't heard any more movement coming from the floor above.

"You okay?" her dad asked.

"Yeah, I'm fine. I'm nannying for the Coopers and I just heard a noise upstairs that sounded like a door closing. But Leo's asleep and there's no one else here. At least, there shouldn't be."

"You think someone's in the house?"

"I don't know. No. I don't think so. The home is gated, they have security cameras, and the doors are locked. I must've heard something else."

"If you hear anything else and think someone has broken in, don't hesitate to call 9-1-1."

"Okay. I'm sure it's nothing."

"Who are the Coopers?"

"Paul and Emily Cooper. You know, the famous actor? Emily is always in the local news for all the charities she's involved in. They hired me to be their nanny for the summer. I told Mom; I thought she would've told you."

There was silence on the other end of the line. Bridgett pulled the phone away from her ear to check if their call had been dropped. It hadn't.

"Dad? Are you still there?"

"I'm here. No, she didn't tell me."

Leo let out a wail through the baby monitor in the back pocket of her shorts.

"I have to go. Leo's crying."

"Okay. Remember what I said about calling 9-1-1 if you need to."

"I will, although I'm sure everything's fine. Love you."

"Love you, too."

CHAPTER TWO

"I feel like we're here with a bunch of super rich people," Blake said.

Tess smiled. "That's because we are."

Blake looked around at the private event's black-tie crowd. "It's a little stuffy for my taste."

"Oh really? Well, aren't you the snob?"

Tess shot him a look that told him she was teasing. She took a sip from her champagne as she admired the view out the Space Needle's floor-to-ceiling windows. "I think it's breathtaking."

Mount Rainier's snow-covered peak was barely visible in the distance as dusk settled over the sky. The downtown skyscrapers and Ferris wheel filled the city with light.

"Yes, it is."

Tess turned to see her boyfriend staring straight at her. "I meant the view."

"So did I," he said with a grin.

He stepped closer to her on the rotating glass floor and placed his arm around her waist. "You should wear this more often."

It had still been daylight when they'd first arrived at the

party and looking down through the glass made it feel as though there was nothing between them and the ground over five hundred feet below. The floor's steady rotation gave them a full 360-degree view of the city every forty-five minutes.

Tess glanced down at her fitted black dress. "I'm not sure this is the look I should be going for when I show up at the scene of a homicide."

"Yeah, I guess not. Maybe you'll just have to wear it around the house."

"Or we could go out more. You know, in all that spare time we have."

Both being homicide detectives, they barely had time to see each other. It had been over month since they'd last gone out on a date.

"I thought your brother was coming tonight," Blake said.

"I forgot to tell you. Apparently, there was an accident on I-90, so he and Chloe are going to be a little late."

"I meant Chris, not Nathan."

"Oh. Yeah, he is. Or at least he said he was. I tried calling him before we got here, but he didn't answer." She looked annoyed.

"I'm sure he's coming," Blake said.

"I hope so. It would be good for him to be here tonight. I really appreciate all the time you've spent with him lately. He looks up to you."

Tess paused and looked pensively at the city below.

"Before my mom died, Chris and I both wanted to be cops. I'd just graduated from the Police Academy when she passed. But Chris was starting college. I think it was harder on him than it was on Nathan and me. We were older and both already had a sense of purpose in life. Nathan had football, and I was at the beginning of a new career. But, ever since she died, Chris has been…lost."

Blake's phone vibrated in his jacket pocket. "It's him," he said, checking the screen.

"Hey, Chris."

"Hey. I tried calling Tess's phone, but she didn't answer. I figured you'd have yours on since you said you were on call."

"She must've turned her phone on silent for the event," Blake said, looking at Tess. "Are you still coming tonight?"

"Yeah, but I'm going to be a little late. I just finished at the Coopers'. I'm going to stop by my apartment to shower and change, then I'll be there. I should get there within the hour."

"Okay, we'll see you soon."

Blake slid his phone into his suit pocket. "He just got done at Paul and Emily's. He's going to stop by his apartment, but he thinks he'll be here within an hour."

"Good," Tess said. "I'm glad he's still coming." She took another sip of champagne. "Did he tell you he has a new girlfriend?"

"No, but that doesn't surprise me. He's seemed happier than usual the last month or so. Is he bringing her tonight?"

She shook her head. "I told him he could, but he said she was working."

"What does she do?"

"I'm not sure."

Blake raised his eyebrows. "Really? I thought you were a better detective than that."

Tess elbowed him playfully in the ribs. "Well, why don't you ask him when he gets here, detective."

He smiled. "Don't worry. I will."

She placed her hand on Blake's forearm. "I'm going to see if I can find Emily. I want to thank her for the invite. And for giving Chris that job for the summer."

Blake glanced at a waiter carrying a tray of hors d'oeuvres through the crowd.

"Sounds good," he said. "I'm going to see if any of the food being served is actually edible."

CHAPTER THREE

Chris dropped his phone into the side pocket of his cargo shorts. He pulled down his tailgate and lifted his weedwhacker into the truck bed. He was already regretting telling Blake he'd go to the party. He had no desire to get dressed up to go stand around, trying to make conversation with a bunch of rich people he didn't know.

Maybe he should call Blake back and tell him he'd changed his mind. He was tired from his long day of work.

He'd never hung out with any of Tess's boyfriends before. He'd only spent time with Blake the first time because Tess wanted them to get to know each other. But he was starting to really like the guy. Some of his badass stories about being a detective were making Chris rethink his career choice as a landscaper.

He closed his tailgate and looked through the front window of the Coopers' mansion. What he really wanted to do was go back inside and spend the rest of the night with his girlfriend. But that wasn't going to happen. So, he might as well go to the stupid party and make his sister happy.

Nathan and Chloe had also said they were going, so at least that would give him a couple other people to talk to.

Although, he hated being introduced to people next to his older brother, who played for the Seahawks.

He could already envision the impressed faces on the wealthy party guests when they learned Nathan played for the team. Then, they'd turn to Chris and politely ask what he did.

Another athlete?

Actually, I'm a landscaper.

There'd be an awkward silence as they tried to pretend that was also fantastic. *Oh well.* He was used to it.

The sound of a throat clearing directly behind him startled him from his thoughts. He spun around.

Once his eyes adjusted on the dark figure in the driveway, he put his hand over his chest.

"Oh," he said, seeing who it was. He felt self-conscious for being so jumpy. "You scared me.

CHAPTER FOUR

Bridgett set her phone on the kitchen island. She headed toward Leo's room as she reached for the monitor. She checked the small screen while she walked down the hall. Seeing him find his pacifier in the crib, she stopped. She waited for him to roll over and go back to sleep before turning for the kitchen to reply to Chris's text.

The granite island was bare when she returned to the kitchen. She was sure she'd left her phone on the counter. Even so, she felt her shorts' pockets just to be sure. She looked around, wondering if she'd absentmindedly set it somewhere else in the kitchen on her way to check on Leo.

She hadn't turned the home's security system back on yet, and she wondered if Chris was playing a trick on her. But she couldn't imagine him doing something like that. Plus, she'd locked the door behind him.

She bent over to check the floor around the kitchen island when a loud static noise came over the baby monitor. Every muscle in her body stiffened as she stared at the small lit-up screen in her hand. Instead of seeing Leo's small sleeping form, a figure wearing a full black ski mask filled the camera's frame.

Bridgett's hands trembled as the ski-masked intruder cocked his head to the side and took slow, deliberate steps toward the camera. The camera shook and the screen went dark as the intruder pulled it from the wall. Once the camera had been readjusted, the ski-masked face filled the screen.

He held a cell phone in front of his mouth, and a computerized voice came through the monitor.

"You can stop looking for your phone. I have it."

He must've been using an app to disguise his voice. Bridgett held down the *Talk* button on her hand-held monitor. "Please—don't hurt Leo."

The masked figure turned his head toward the boy's crib. "He's fine. At least he will be if you do exactly what I say."

She blinked through her tears and pressed the *Talk* button again. "I'll do whatever you want. Don't hurt him— please!"

The camera moved away from the ski-masked face and panned to the side. It stopped, focusing on the large blade in the man's gloved hand.

"That is entirely up to you," the computerized voice said.

Bridgett looked around the home for a way to alert the police. She crept toward the circular black device atop the fireplace mantle in the adjoining living room.

"Alexa," she whispered as she moved past the baby grand piano.

The small black circle didn't light up like she'd expected. Bridgett took a few steps closer to the fireplace.

"*Alexa! Call 9-1-1!*" Afraid to alert the ski-masked intruder, she raised the volume of her voice only slightly.

This time the circle lit up in response to her voice, but it turned red instead of green.

"Sorry, I'm having trouble connecting to the internet.

Take a look at the help section in your Alexa app," Alexa's voice resounded through the living room.

Bridgett looked at the monitor screen in her hand and watched the ski-masked man turn his head in response to Alexa's voice. Bridgett ran toward the fireplace. Standing next to the device, she said, "Alexa, turn volume to four."

"I'm offline at the moment. Please try again later."

Bridgett's heart raced as she watched the intruder bring the phone up to his mouth on the monitor's small screen. His computerized voice came through the speaker.

"You're not listening." He lifted the long blade and pointed the tip toward the camera. "I've disabled the WiFi. No one is coming to save you. If you try calling for help again, the boy dies."

She pressed the *Talk* button. "I won't. I'll do whatever you say."

"Good."

"Let me see him. I need to know that you haven't already hurt him."

Bridgett stood still as the camera spun across the room and hovered over Leo's crib. She exhaled deeply when she saw his sweet sleeping form. The camera moved to the child's side, and she could see the slow, even rise and fall of the boy's chest. A moment later, the camera blurred. The ski mask filled the screen again.

"Satisfied?"

Bridgett nodded even though he couldn't see her. She lifted the monitor closer to her mouth. "Yes. What do you want me to do?"

The computerized voice crackled through the monitor. "I want the necklace."

Bridgett thought about playing dumb. She could ask

what necklace he was talking about. She wondered, though, what good that would do her. She couldn't risk the boy's life. And, she knew exactly what necklace he'd come to steal.

Bridgett had seen it for the first time that evening. She'd been helping Emily lay out her dress in her two-story, custom walk-in closet for tomorrow night's benefit gala. Her jaw fell open when Emily pulled the exquisite piece of jewelry from the safe. She wanted to see how it would look against the pale-yellow designer gown that she planned to wear for the prestigious event.

A string of white diamonds held up a large yellow stone on either side.

"It's a yellow diamond," Emily said, seeing Bridgett's mouth gaping open. "One of the largest Asscher cut diamonds in the world."

Bridgett watched in awe as Emily casually held the necklace up to her dress.

"It's just over 75 carats."

Emily turned to the full-length mirror and lifted the gleaming heirloom to her neck. Bridgett was speechless.

"The necklace belonged to Paul's late mother," Emily told her.

Emily had never mentioned Paul's mother before, but it was common knowledge that she'd been a famous actress. It was how Paul had gotten his start in acting.

"It was gifted to her in the 1960s by her second husband. He was a billionaire Texas oil tycoon. They divorced two years later. She could've sold it for millions, but she never did."

Emily looked unimpressed with the necklace when Bridgett caught her reflection in the mirror. The look was gone from her face when Emily turned and set the jewels on top of the white dresser in the middle of the closet.

"I better get going so we aren't late to the party."

Emily slipped on a pair of Christian Louboutin stilettos, making her nearly a foot taller than Bridgett. She looked in the mirror one more time. Bridgett felt frumpy in her plaid shirt and cutoff shorts as she watched Emily straighten her white minidress and ruffle her dark auburn curls.

Emily led the way out of the room.

"You don't want to put the necklace back in the safe?" Bridgett asked.

"I want to make sure to wear it tomorrow. I don't get the chance very often. The closet is the most secure room of the house. No one can get in without the key code."

Bridgett followed Emily into her master bedroom. She heard the closet door lock behind her. Emily lowered her voice and turned to Bridgett before going downstairs where her husband waited to take her to their annual private event for their non-profit organization.

"Plus, it's insured. But don't tell Paul I said that." A smile escaped Emily's lips. "He's sentimental about it."

From the look on Emily's face, she seemed to think it was silly her husband would be sentimental about a one-of-a-kind, multi-million-dollar designer necklace that had belonged to his late mother.

"Okay."

"We have a lot of big donors to thank tonight. Some of them really like to party. And we'll be watching the fireworks from the Space Needle. So, I doubt we'll be home before two."

"No problem. Have a good time."

Bridgett wasn't sure how many millions the necklace was worth, but Emily had told her its value was more than the

Seattle waterfront estate she was standing in.

She pressed the *Talk* button. She had helped Emily pack for an overnight trip last week, and she knew the code for the closet. As long as it hadn't changed.

"I can get it. But how do I know you won't hurt him after I give it to you?"

Static came through the speakers before his response. "You don't. But, if you don't get it for me, I promise that both you and the boy won't live through the night."

Bridgett swallowed hard. *What choice did she have?*

"There's a black duffel bag by the front door. Take the bag, put the necklace inside, and return it to where you found it. Then, go to the kitchen and wait for me to leave. I'll be taking your phone with me to ensure you don't call for help before I'm gone."

Bridgett took slow steps toward the hallway that led to the entryway.

"Tell me you understand."

She was startled by the computerized voice coming through the monitor louder than it had before.

"I understand," she said.

The home's original hardwood floor creaked under her bare feet as she crept down the hall.

Her eyes fixed on the alarm system on the wall above the empty duffel bag. The rectangular, white box had been ripped from the wall, exposing a triad of colored wires. As she came closer, she saw that every wire in the security system had been severed. With shaking hands, she reached for the duffel bag.

Light coming through the window next to the front door caused her to turn as she stood up with the bag. It wasn't the front porch lights. They were off. Even though they were always timed to go on in the evening. It looked like the headlights from Chris's truck. *Thank God.*

She nearly jumped in the air from the sound of a door closing upstairs. She turned but saw only the vacant staircase. She stood still for a few moments, knowing Leo's room was at the end of the lengthy upstairs hallway.

Her breathing quickened when the masked intruder appeared at the top of the stairs. The black balaclava covered his entire face. He wore a black hooded sweatshirt with dark pants and lace-up boots.

He took one step down the stairs and rested his gloved hand atop the banister, showing off the long blade of his knife. She was glad to see it was free of blood, a sign he hadn't hurt Leo. He pointed the tip of the blade toward Emily and Paul's bedroom door.

Bridgett wondered what the odds were that he wouldn't kill her after she got the necklace for him. This kind of break-in had required an incredible amount of skill and planning. *What if he killed Leo after she got him what he wanted?* Although she couldn't see his face, she had the feeling he was every bit a psychopath. Something in her gut told her he wasn't going to let them live.

He was far enough away from Leo's room that she decided to take the chance. It seemed their best shot at survival. She could get Chris's attention and get back inside before the burglar got to Leo. Hopefully, the maniac would chase after her.

Chris was strong. And, he had a cell phone and a truck.

Bridgett dropped the bag and flung open the solid wood door.

CHAPTER FIVE

"Chris!"

She ran straight for the headlights. She squinted from the bright beams as she got closer to the truck.

"Chris! Help me! There's a man in the house!"

She slammed her fist on the hood as she ran past it to the driver's door. The inside of his truck was dark. She yanked the door open. The interior lights came on, but the cab was empty.

She turned to check if the intruder had followed her. He hadn't. She was alone in the eerily quiet driveway. She knew she didn't have much time if she was going to get back inside before the creep got to Leo.

Where was Chris? It didn't make any sense.

"Chris!"

She ran to the rear of his truck. She had just rounded the corner behind his rear bumper when she tripped and fell to the ground. Her palms broke her fall, skidding atop the stamped concrete. She got to her knees and turned around.

Her stomach churned when she realized what she had tripped over. Her boyfriend lay on the driveway behind his truck. He was both silent and still.

"Chris—" Her voice came out as a whimper. She crawled closer to him. Her hands dipped into a lukewarm puddle as she neared his head. "Oh, no. No, no!"

She knelt over him and placed a hand over either side of his face. Her eyes had adjusted to the dark enough to see that his throat had been slit deeply.

"Chris!" she screamed again as if she could wake him up.

He didn't respond. She lay her head on his chest, praying to hear a heartbeat. But there was nothing.

She sat up, choking back her tears. Leo. She had to go inside before that maniac killed him too.

She wiped her hands on her plaid, button-up shirt as she stood. She stepped on something hard next to Chris's body and bent down to pick it up. She felt sick when her hand gripped the handle of the bloody knife. The knife that killed Chris.

A light from the house caught her attention. She stepped out from behind Chris's truck. Her eyes focused on the dark figure standing on the home's grand front porch. The balaclava still covered his face. His feet were planted hip-width apart. He stared back at her, holding little Leo in his arm.

Leo was awake, but, surprisingly, he wasn't crying. He calmly sucked his pacifier next to the masked stranger. Seeing the child in the killer's arms sent a surge of anger through her body. She watched the madman lift his phone to his lips.

His computerized voice echoed through the phone's speaker in the quiet, private drive. "Come back inside. Or the child dies. Leave the knife where you found it."

She watched the man turn and take the child inside. Bridgett was left alone in the secluded driveway with her boyfriend's dead body. She picked up the baby monitor from the ground and looked at Chris one last time before she walked back into the house.

CHAPTER SIX

The monitor lit up in Bridgett's hand once she stepped inside the house.

"Close the door behind you," the killer's voice said.

She could tell from the monitor's screen that he had returned to Leo's room. She did as she was told.

"Now, pick up the bag and go get the necklace. Or you and the boy will end up just like your boyfriend."

She clenched her jaw and grabbed the duffel bag with her blood-stained hand. She tucked the monitor into the back pocket of her shorts and climbed the stairs to the master bedroom.

She passed the blue and yellow Victor Vasarely painting that hung halfway up the stairwell. She'd learned about the European artist in the art class she'd taken freshman year. She'd been amazed to see one of his originals in someone's private home when she'd come for her interview over a month before. Seeing her gawking at the well-known piece of Op art, Emily had told her they'd won it at a charity auction.

She entered the master bedroom and approached the locked door to Emily's walk-in closet. She reached for the keypad, but her hand froze before she typed in the code. What if Emily had changed the code since giving it to her last weekend?

Bridgett took in a deep breath and punched in the code she'd used last week. There was an audible click from the door's locking mechanism. Bridgett exhaled and opened the closet door. The recessed lighting automatically came on as she entered the large space.

The glimmering necklace was exactly where Emily had left it. Bridgett carefully lifted the heirloom off the dresser and laid it inside the duffel bag. She zipped the bag closed and hurried downstairs. She set the bag on the floor by the front door and pulled the blood-stained monitor from her back pocket.

She pressed Talk. She fought the urge to vomit at the sight of Chris's dried blood on the monitor as well as her hands. "I got it. The necklace is in the bag by the front door."

The ski-masked face reappeared on the small screen. "Good girl. The Coopers are lucky to have such a caring nanny for their son. Go to the kitchen and wait for me to leave. After I'm gone, you can check on the boy."

Bridgett let the monitor fall to her side. She couldn't bring herself to respond to the homicidal stranger as she walked through the large home to the kitchen. She heard Leo's bedroom door close upstairs.

There were more lights on in the kitchen than when she'd left it. A large newspaper clipping lay on the kitchen island where Bridgett had last seen her phone. She felt a chill run down the back of her neck as she slowly moved toward the newspaper article.

A bold headline filled the top of the page: Seattle

Freshman Wins Regional Gymnastic Championship. She recognized the photo immediately. She'd been fourteen when she won the competition.

She wore a long-sleeve blue and red leotard and beamed for the camera. Her parents framed her on either side. They were so proud. Bridgett held a small bouquet of flowers next to the Regionals' medal that hung around her neck. Her blonde hair was pulled into a tight bun atop her head.

She had no idea why Chris's killer would have put this article in the kitchen for her to find. She lifted her head and looked around the room. She hadn't heard the thief leave through the front door like he'd said. She focused on her surroundings and heard the faint, rhythmic sound of the soles of his boots treading slowing down the hallway toward the kitchen.

She scanned the kitchen for something she could use to defend herself. There was nothing on the bare countertops that could serve as a weapon. She looked up, her eyes drawn to the pots and pans hanging above the kitchen island. The footsteps grew closer.

She glanced at the article as she backed away from the kitchen island. The masked madman hadn't come for the necklace at all. She had no idea why, but he'd come for her.

CHAPTER SEVEN

There was nowhere to hide. The footsteps had almost reached the doorway to the kitchen. Bridgett reached for the handle of a large cast-iron pan. In her panic to pull it down, the pan caught on the edge of the metal hook that suspended it.

The footsteps rounded the doorway behind her. She let go of the handle and dove to the floor. The pan swung like a clock pendulum and clamored against the other hanging pots and pans.

Bridgett crawled behind the kitchen island. She scanned the dining and living room for a better hiding spot. She heard the killer's boots enter the kitchen. Seeing no better option, she scurried on all fours to the dining room and tucked under the dining table.

She tried to quiet her breathing as she looked toward the kitchen. The killer stood behind the island. He reached his gloved hand in the air to still the pan that was clanging against the other pots. He didn't appear to see her under the table. He turned around as if he'd heard a noise behind him.

Bridgett watched him walk straight toward the pantry door and pull it open. Seeing it was empty, he turned and marched past the kitchen island toward the living room.

It wouldn't take long for him to find her. There weren't many places to hide.

She could only see him now from the waist down. The blade in his left hand looked even bigger up close. She focused on his boots. They moved in the direction of the dining room. Bridgett's heart beat so hard against her chest she was afraid the killer would hear it. His feet stopped when he'd halfway closed the distance between them. Bridgett watched them turn away from her, and she knew it was now or never.

She scooted out from under the table, crouched down, and ran for the walk-in pantry. She half expected to feel the knife in her back as she ran. But she made it. He'd left the door wide open. She stepped inside and pulled the door closed, stopping before it latched and leaving it open a crack.

She held her breath and watched his silhouette through the pantry door's frosted glass. Thankfully, his back was to her. Bridgett watched him turn his head as he searched the living room. He checked the dining room to his left before turning around to face the kitchen. He seemed to be scanning the kitchen when his face came to a stop. He stared directly into the pantry door.

Bridgett ran her hands along the darkened shelves and closed her grip around what felt like a can of soup.

He came toward the pantry, slow and deliberate. She pressed her body against the shelving. His dark form came to a stop in front of the pantry door. He stared into the frosted glass. As he reached for the door handle, Bridgett closed her eyes for a split second and prepared to have the fight of her life.

The door swung open. Bridgett took a step back. He raised the knife with both hands and swung the blade at Bridgett's chest. She turned reflexively, feeling the sharp metal slice into her left triceps and upper back. As soon as she felt the blade pull away from her skin, she pivoted.

Ignoring the pain from her wound, Bridgett slammed the bottom of the can into the side of the ski-masked face. The killer stumbled backward, holding his long, bloodied blade in one hand. Bridgett ran past him.

She jumped onto the kitchen island and grabbed the handle of the cast iron pan as the killer's cold, gloved hand encircled her ankle. She jerked the pan from its hook as her body was pulled to the kitchen floor.

The cut on her back stung when she hit the hardwood floor. She looked up at the killer, who was now kneeling on either side of her waist. He lifted the knife above his head. Full of adrenaline, Bridgett squeezed the handle of the cast-iron pan and struck his head as hard as she could.

The blow knocked the ski-masked intruder to the floor. He fell beside her, stunned, but Bridgett didn't know for how long. She jumped to her feet and ran out of the kitchen to find Leo.

Trembling from her adrenaline rush, she took the corner to the hallway too fast for her weak muscles. She stumbled to the side and fell against the wall. She quickly regained her momentum and ran the rest of the way to the stairwell. The black duffel bag lay untouched by the front door.

"Leo! Are you okay? I'm coming for you, baby! It's gonna be all right."

Bridgett glanced over her shoulder when she reached the stairs. No ski mask. At least not yet. She took the stairs two at a time.

In her hurry to get away from him, she'd left the pan on the floor of the kitchen. Now, she realized, she had nothing left to defend herself with.

"Leo!"

She was out of breath when she got to his room. She slowed, seeing his bedroom door was halfway open. There was no noise coming from the boy's room. She was filled with terror of what she was going to find.

"Leo?" she asked softly from the doorway.

There was no response. She flicked on the lights. To her relief, his crib was empty. It was better than the scenario she had imagined. But now she was filled with a new fear. Where was he? What had that monster done with him?

She turned and went out to the hall. "Leo!" she screamed.

She ran to the next room down the hall, but the door handle wouldn't budge. She jiggled the wrought-iron handle back and forth to no avail. She slammed her palm against the door.

"Leo? Are you in there sweetie?" Again, no response.

She ran to the next room. Just as before, the door was locked and there was no response on the inside from Leo. She raced to Paul and Emily's bedroom door. The door she had gone through to get the necklace. She tried the door. But it too was locked. She slammed her side against the door. She winced from the pain from her knife wound.

"Leo!"

Ignoring the sting in her back, she pressed her body against the door when she saw the ski mask coming up the stairs. Her desperation to save the boy's life overrode any fear she held for her own. She came forward and leaned over the banister, glaring at the masked psychopath.

"Where is he?"

The killer didn't respond and continued to climb the stairs. He looked blurry through the tears that filled her eyes.

Bridgett didn't retreat as the ski mask advanced. "What have you done to him?"

He ascended the stairs in silence.

Bridgett's rage for the child's life overtook her. "Where is he?" she screamed.

The killer stopped, one step from the top. He was close enough that Bridgett could tell his eyes were blue. He could've killed her if he wanted. But he didn't. Instead, he pointed his knife toward the end of the hall past Paul and Emily's room. Bridgett turned and ran to the last room off the upstairs hallway.

The door opened easily.

CHAPTER EIGHT

"Who let you two in here?"

The two detectives turned to see Tess's brother and sister-in-law walking toward them. They both held a glass of champagne and her brother flashed them a look of amusement at his own joke. Blake had gotten to know the Seahawk and his wife over the last five months he and Tess had been dating.

The women exchanged a hug.

Nathan gave Blake a friendly slap on the shoulder. "Good to see you."

The defensive lineman and homicide detective were almost the same height, but Nathan had about fifty extra pounds of muscle.

"You too."

Nathan lifted his glass toward Blake's Diet Coke. "No champagne?"

"I'm on call."

"Still? I thought you were on call the last time I saw you. What was that, two weeks ago? Well, I guess that's a good thing. It means no one's been murdered yet, right?"

"Right."

"You guys didn't see Chris on your way up did you?" Tess asked.

"No," Chloe said. "We thought he'd be here already."

"He's coming," Blake said. "He called almost an hour ago and said he'd gotten off work late. He should be here any minute."

"Sounds like Chris," Nathan said.

Chloe looked down at her feet. "This floor is amazing. I bet it's even more terrifying in the daylight. I guess that's partly why the renovation cost so much. I remember reading they spent close to one hundred million on it. Do you guys mind if we go outside? I want to check it out."

"Sure," Tess said.

The four of them stepped out onto the observation deck. Although it was fully enclosed, the glass panels made it feel like there was nothing between them and the city below.

"I got some good news yesterday," Nathan said after they'd all admired the view. "The Seahawks renewed my contract, so it looks like you guys will be seeing a little more of us."

"That's awesome!" Tess exclaimed.

"Yeah, that's great," Blake said. "Congratulations."

Nathan put his muscular arm around his wife. "Thanks. We're really happy about it. I'd been pretty sure they were going to re-sign me, but it's nice for it to finally be official."

"Cheers to that," Tess said.

Blake raised his Diet Coke with their three champagne glasses. "Cheers."

"Maybe we should head inside," Tess said once they'd all taken a drink. "It looks like Paul's getting ready to give a speech."

"Hopefully our little brother will make it before the party's over," Nathan said.

He and Chloe led the way. After they'd gone inside, Blake held the door open for Tess to follow.

"Thanks," Tess said as she went through the doorway. She checked her phone before putting it back in her purse, making sure she hadn't missed a call from Chris.

CHAPTER NINE

Bridgett had never been in this room before. Never had any reason to be. She'd always assumed it was a guest room.

The lights were already on. Bridgett closed the door behind her and locked it, even though it hadn't seemed the ski-masked monster had bothered to follow her. It made her wonder if she'd walked into a trap.

The room was bare except for an upholstered chair. A faded 4x6 photo lay in the middle of the seat. Her eyes moved to the large red letters on the wall beside the chair. GO DOWN TO THEATER. At first, she thought the words had been written in blood. But, as she moved closer, she could tell it was spray paint.

She turned to the closed closet doors behind her.

"Leo?"

She opened the doors. The closet was bare, aside from a bag of golf clubs that leaned against the wall. She pulled a club from the bag. She held it at her side as she crossed the room and picked up the photo from the chair.

The madman could've killed her on the stairs, but he didn't. Why? He didn't even try. She'd gotten away from him downstairs, but Bridgett doubted she would have come out the winner against another attack.

There were three people in the photograph, but only one she recognized. Her father. She stared at the photo, confused. They looked like a happy family. But that couldn't be possible. He was never married before her mother, and Bridgett was an only child.

In the photo, her father had his arm around a redheaded woman. They were both smiling. His other arm held a little girl with strawberry blonde pigtails. She appeared to be laughing. She looked no older than three.

Bridgett flipped the photo over in her hand. 1992 was handwritten in blue ink on the top right corner. She looked across at the locked door that led to the hall, wondering why the killer hadn't tried to come in after her. Was he waiting outside the door to kill her? Or block her in and set the house on fire? What did he want from her?

She turned the picture over in her hand and stared closer at the happy threesome. What did it mean?

She folded the photo in half and tucked it into the front pocket of her shorts. For the first time, she noticed the fresh blood dripping down the side of her left leg. She reached her arm behind her shoulder and felt her sliced skin where her shirt had been ripped by the killer's blade. The cut stung from the sweat on her fingers. She pulled her hand away and wiped the blood on her fingertips against her thigh.

Regardless of what the photo meant, she had to find Leo. And get him out of the home safely. She unlocked the French doors that led to an outside balcony. The wood deck felt cool on her bare feet as she walked to the edge.

Goosebumps formed up her legs from the cool breeze coming off Lake Washington at the end of the two-acre property. Bright, booming fireworks lit up the dark sky from a show put on by another mansion two houses down. There was no chance any of the far-off neighbors would hear her cries for help.

Bridgett peered over the wrought-iron railing to the in-ground pool three stories below. She was confident she could reach it if she jumped. But she couldn't leave Leo here alone. Not with that monster. She'd never forgive herself if Leo died before she was able to get help.

She went inside and closed the door behind her. She looked again at the writing on the wall. What was waiting for her in the basement theater? Hopefully, Leo. A living and breathing Leo. She was ready to give her life for his if she had to. She prayed the masked maniac would let him live.

Her hand trembled as she unlocked the door to the hall. She gripped the golf club like a baseball bat before swinging the door open.

She felt her heart race when she stepped out into the empty hallway. She looked over her shoulder as she crept toward the stairs, wondering if the message was just a trick to lure her out of the room.

There was still no sign of the ski mask when she started down the stairs. Her grip remained tight around the golf club as she descended. She choked back her tears, seeing Chris's headlights still glowing in the driveway.

She rounded the second flight of stairs leading to the daylight basement. She had a sinking feeling in the pit of her stomach as she neared the bottom. It was hard to imagine how this night could end well.

The basement was comfortably lit by various lamps that were set to go on by timers. She moved with careful steps past the bar and the door to the wine cellar. She saw the lights from the pool through the windows that led to the garden patio. She walked past the billiard table on her way to the theater.

A dim blue light flashed though the theater's doorway. Bridgett froze before entering the room.

Knowing she had no choice, she moved her feet, one after the other. She did her best to stifle the fear growing inside her. She exhaled after crossing through the theater's doorway. No ski mask.

But there was no Leo either. The large flat screen was on. The word SIT filled the screen in black letters against a white background. Bridgett looked around before taking the first leather recliner on her left.

Moments after she'd taken her seat, a slide show began to play. No music. Just photos. The pictures made the hair on her arms stand up.

There was a photo of her with a silver medal at another regional gymnastic meet with both her parents. Photos of both her high school and college graduations. A photo of the modest home she grew up in. The home where her parents still lived. A photo her dad had posted on Facebook last spring. He had his arm around her, and Bridgett held up her acceptance letter to dental school. There was a picture of her getting out of her Honda Accord at UW.

The slideshow ended with the same faded photograph of her father and the two redheads that Bridgett had folded into her pocket. The longer she looked at the little girl's blue eyes, the more certain she was of her identity. She was surprised she hadn't seen it earlier.

When the killer stood one stair down from her, they were almost the same height. And Emily was twenty-nine, which would make her the right age to be the girl in the photo.

Bridgett was born three years after that photo had been taken. And her parents had met in the fall of 1992. From the clothes they wore, the picture looked to have been taken during summer.

All her life, she'd known her father to be a kind, decent man. How could he have had another daughter and never told her? Emily couldn't be my father's daughter. There was no way he would've kept that from me and mom. But the photo didn't lie.

Before she could think of an answer to her own questions, her thoughts were interrupted. Bridgett jumped in her seat as the familiar female voice came through the surround sound.

CHAPTER TEN

"Good evening, everyone."

Tess and Blake turned to see Emily's husband, Paul, standing on a small platform with a microphone in his hand. Although Blake had met Paul briefly at a charity event with Tess a few months back, he mostly recognized him from the famous sitcom he'd starred in a decade earlier. Blake guessed Paul was over sixty, but he looked like he hadn't aged since his years on TV. His lean build was obvious through his suit, and, even with his white hair, there was a youthfulness about him.

"On behalf of both Emily and I, I wanted to thank you all for coming tonight to celebrate the breast cancer research we've been able to fund through The Cooper Foundation. Unfortunately, Emily was called away for family reasons at the start of the party. She wished she could've stayed. Your generosity to our foundation means the world to her."

"I thought you talked to her earlier?" Blake whispered into Tess's ear.

"No." She leaned in closer to him. "I forgot to tell you. I've been so distracted by Chris not showing up."

It had been over an hour since Blake had spoken to him

on the phone. They had both tried calling him before Paul's speech, but he wasn't answering.

"I only talked to Paul, and he told me Emily had gone home sick. It seemed really unlike her. Their foundation is so important to her."

Having both lost their mothers to breast cancer, Tess and Emily had formed an instant bond when they met through The Cooper Foundation two years ago.

"There are a few people in particular Emily wanted me to make sure to thank this evening," Paul continued. "The first is Detective Tess Richards."

Blake placed his hand on the small of her back, knowing she was every bit deserving of the thanks she was about to get. He had never met a woman he more admired. She was also incredibly beautiful. She looked like a model in her black dress with her long blonde hair pulled back into an elegant bun.

"I know this is a cause that is close to your heart since your mother passed away from breast cancer. The time and effort you've put forth to help raise money for this research has made a huge impact, and you are an inspiration to both Emily and me."

Paul went on to specifically thank a few of the foundation's biggest donors. He concluded by thanking everyone for their contributions and for coming to tonight's event.

Tess turned to Blake as Paul stepped off the platform. "It's really weird that she left."

"Who? Emily? I thought she was sick."

"Yeah, I guess. But missing tonight's event would've been the last thing she wanted. She's been planning it for months. I saw her talking to some people when we first got here. She looked different. Distracted."

"Maybe she didn't feel good." Blake stuffed the second half of his bacon-wrapped jalapeno popper into his mouth.

"Maybe."

"I think you should just enjoy tonight and stop worrying so much about everybody else. I want to celebrate you." He grinned. "As soon as I get back from the bathroom. I have to pee."

Tess laughed as she watched him walk away. She pulled her phone out of her clutch to see if Chris had called or texted her. Nothing. She checked the time. He should've been there by now.

Nathan and Chloe had gone to the bar for a second round of drinks. She wasn't sure how much Nathan donated to The Cooper Foundation, but she was sure it was a lot. He was as dedicated to helping other families affected by the disease as she was.

Tess stepped outside onto the glass-paneled observation deck to try calling Chris again. Although it was dark, she could see the lights from the boats that filled Lake Union, waiting to watch the fireworks display. Chris's phone rang four times before going to his voicemail.

She'd tell Blake when he got back from the bathroom that she wanted to stop by Chris's apartment. It wasn't far from the Space Needle.

CHAPTER ELEVEN

"He never told you about us, did he?"

Without the voice distortion, Bridgett immediately recognized her voice. Having no way to respond, Bridgett stood from the chair and waited for Emily to continue.

"That doesn't surprise me. That son of a bitch you call a father never even had the decency to send me a birthday card after he left us for your mother. It was as if we were dead to him."

Although she recognized Emily's voice, it sounded different. There was a distinct viciousness in her tone that Bridgett had never heard before.

"I was only three when he left. Only three when he met your mother and decided he loved her so much he never wanted to see me or my mother again."

At least, Bridgett thought, if Emily was the one behind the ski mask, that should mean that Leo was safe. Right?

"I would've included more photos of my childhood in the slide show, but I'm afraid the only happy memories I have are before our father left."

Bridgett racked her brain for any memories that would've suggested her father had a child before he'd met her mother, but she had nothing. Maybe Emily was lying. She was obviously crazy. But there was no mistaking Bridgett's father in that photo.

"He killed my mother. After he left, her one glass of wine every night turned into drinking herself to sleep. Three years later, she drank herself to death. I was only six the morning I couldn't wake her up to take me to school.

"I know Paul told you my mother died of breast cancer, but he doesn't know the truth. That was just a lie. It was what I needed to get accepted into the rich, exclusive charity world in this town, which was how I met Paul.

"Anyway, since the state was unable to contact my father, I was put into the foster system. I lived in five homes over the next twelve years. It wasn't horrific, but I was never truly loved. I was always an outsider. A misfit. A temporary guest in another family's home, rather than belonging. Meanwhile, you were born to two loving, doting parents who gave you everything you could've ever wanted. A father who managed to make every major gymnastic meet you had despite his busy job. But there was no room in his life for me. My father, your father, robbed me of a loving family and a happy home."

Bridgett clenched the rubber grip of the golf club. She walked out of the theater.

Emily continued to speak through the surround sound. "He's a monster. A selfish bastard. And none of you deserve to be happy."

Bridgett walked slowly, expecting Emily to jump out from behind the furniture and attack her. Bridgett edged past the billiard table. She stopped and turned when she felt a cold wind on her legs.

Emily stood just beyond the opened patio doors. She'd

removed the ski mask but still wore the oversized black sweatshirt, pants, and work boots that disguised her feminine frame. Her long auburn hair cascaded past her shoulders. She'd removed all the makeup she'd worn earlier to the party. It was why Bridgett hadn't recognized her earlier, when she'd looked into her eyes on the stairs.

Seeing the long blade in Emily's hand, Bridgett sensed she'd made the wrong decision. She should've gone for help instead of trying to find Leo on her own. There was no chance she could overpower Emily.

Bridgett was still in good shape from all her years in gymnastics, but she wasn't as strong as Emily. Not only was Emily over six inches taller than her, but the woman worked out every day and kept herself in exceptional shape.

"I don't know why it surprised me to learn you were going to dental school. Daddy's little girl. Following in daddy's footsteps."

"What do you want from me?" Bridgett asked.

Emily scoffed. "I want you to suffer. Suffer like I've suffered. Experience what it feels like to feel abandoned and afraid. Then I'm going to take your life away from you. Just like you and your mother took my life away from me. It won't change my childhood or bring back my mother, but at least I can watch you die in agony. That will have to be enough."

"Where is Leo?"

"Oh, please. My son is none of your concern."

"Does Paul know about this?"

"Of course not. He thinks I came home sick from the party. He won't be home for another couple hours. Plenty of time for me to carry out my plans for you. He'll be shocked to learn when he comes home that you killed your boyfriend and tried to steal his mother's necklace. And that I had to kill you in self-defense before you killed my son."

"No one's going to believe that," Bridgett said. "They'll find evidence you did it."

Emily smiled. "Really? Because I think your fingerprints are on the necklace and the keypad to my closet. You're the only one who knew the necklace wasn't in the safe. And, you were even dumb enough to pick up the knife that killed Chris.

"Are you wondering how I found you?" Emily continued.

She wasn't. She was too focused on poor little Leo.

"I hired a private investigator after I married Paul. One of the perks of having a rich husband. When I learned you were a student at UW, I decided to create a summer nanny position on their job site with enough financial compensation to hopefully attract your attention. And it worked. I had about three hundred other applicants before your name came through."

Emily stretched her neck to one side and then the other.

"Anyway, I think that's enough chit chat for one night, don't you?"

Bridgett didn't know how to respond. Emily grinned. She lifted the knife in her hand and lunged toward her.

CHAPTER TWELVE

Blake had almost reached the curved stairwell that led to the upstairs bathrooms when an elderly woman stepped into his path. He stopped abruptly to keep from running into her. She eyed him intensely and reached out her heavily-jeweled hand to shake his.

"I'm Norma."

Her bright red nail polish was a perfect match to her lipstick.

He returned her handshake. "I'm Blake."

It hadn't seemed possible for her to step any closer, but she did. Her lips remained fixed in a smile. He quietly cleared his throat from the potency of her perfume.

"I heard you're a homicide detective."

He nodded. "That's right."

Her eyes were wide with fascination, as if they'd shared a dirty secret. Blake felt her hand grip his arm.

"I've always been intrigued by murder. Tell me, detective. Between you and me, what's the worst thing you've ever seen?"

In the two years he'd been a homicide detective, she wasn't the first person to ask him something like this at a social event. And he was sure she wouldn't be the last.

"Um. I'm sorry, will you excuse me? I was just on my way to the bathroom." He gave a polite smile and moved past her, pulling his arm out of her hold. "It was nice to meet you."

She made no effort to hide her disappointment as her eyes followed him until he was out of her sight.

On his way back downstairs, Blake appreciated the Space Needle's architecture as he slowly descended the staircase. He hadn't been to the Needle since he was a kid. Since its renovation earlier that year, the structure was even more impressive than he had remembered.

He scanned the crowd below and was happy to see his murder-obsessed friend had taken another guest captive in conversation. Hopefully he could find Tess without her seeing him.

He felt someone bump into him from behind, and Blake reached for the handrail to steady himself. He turned to see Paul, looking distracted with his phone in his hand.

"Sorry," Paul said.

"That's all right."

"It's Blake, right? You're Tess's boyfriend?"

Blake could tell Paul was trying to be polite even though he was obviously preoccupied by something else.

Blake nodded. "Yeah, that's right."

Paul looked down again at his phone. "I was just checking our home's security cameras and they're all down. This has never happened before. I can't get a hold of Emily or our nanny. I'm going home. I need to make sure they're all right."

"Do you want Tess and I to follow you?"

"Oh, no. No, that's okay," Paul said as he moved down

the stairs. "But thank you."

Blake watched Paul walk to the elevator before he continued down the stairs to find Tess.

"Blake."

He turned toward the sound of his girlfriend's voice. She had just come inside from the observation deck and moved quickly in his direction.

"I just ran into Paul." Blake told her about his home security cameras not working. "I offered to follow him home, but he said no."

"Had Chris already left their house when you talked to him earlier?"

"I don't know. He just said he was leaving. Although, it didn't sound like he was driving. So, maybe he was about to."

"Something's not right." She grabbed Blake by the arm. "Let's go."

CHAPTER THIRTEEN

Bridgett dashed for the billiard table. Emily followed, and Bridgett jumped on top of the table. She swung the club at Emily's head as she approached. Emily leaned back as the club came within an inch of her face.

Bridgett took another swing. This time, Emily saw it coming. She grabbed the club and lifted the large knife in her other hand. She simultaneously pulled on the club and thrust the blade toward Bridgett's chest.

Bridgett let go of the club and fell onto the table as the blade grazed the front of her shirt. She grabbed the cue ball and threw it at Emily's head.

Emily ducked to the side and the ball missed her by several inches. She let out a playful laugh. Bridgett stood to her feet.

"Come on, little sis. You can do better than that." She took the knife and swung it across the table at Bridgett's bare legs.

Bridgett impulsively threw her body backward. The blade swiped through the air under her feet as she went into a backflip. She put her arms out to her sides to steady herself when she landed on the edge of the table.

"That's better," Emily grinned.

Bridgett felt sick to her stomach at the look of enjoyment on Emily's face. Emily moved around the side of the table. Her eyes were fixed on Bridgett's as she moved in her direction.

Bridgett waited for Emily to get closer before she reached for the cue stick at her feet. Emily was halfway down the table when Bridgett grasped the cue stick and shoved the end of it into Emily's throat.

Emily bent over the table and raised her hand to her neck. Bridgett heard her draw in a series of short, hoarse gasps as Bridgett ran to the end of the table and jumped onto the basement floor. She scooped the golf club off the carpet.

Emily turned toward her, her hand still clutching her throat. Bridgett bolted out the opened door to the garden patio.

To her disadvantage, the pool area was well lit. Emily was only seconds behind her. Bridgett scanned the patio for a place to hide. She tucked behind an imported palm tree near the side of the house. Fireworks were exploding in the midnight sky over the lake.

"I think I've had nearly enough fun for one evening," Emily's voice came through the basement door. "Now it's time for you to get what you deserve."

Bridgett heard Emily's boots step across the concrete patio. The footsteps grew closer and Emily's shadow appeared on the other side of the palm tree. Bridgett saw from the shadow that Emily still held the knife in her hand. Bridgett tightened her grip on the golf club and waited for Emily to move in front of the tree. Bridgett's body tensed as she prepared to move. She would only have one shot at hitting a small target.

Bridgett stepped out from behind the palm and swung the club as hard as she could at Emily's hands. She felt the club make contact before hearing the blade skid across the concrete patio. Emily turned in the direction of her fallen weapon. Bridgett lifted the club over her shoulder as Emily turned back to face her.

Bridgett was mid-swing when Emily wrapped both arms around her chest, forcing her to take several steps backward to maintain her balance. Bridgett felt the curved edge of the pool on the ball of her bare foot before she fell into the water.

She held her breath as Emily's weight on her chest kept her submerged. Bridgett kicked and flailed, fighting to get to the surface. She felt for Emily's hands on her back and attempted to pry them off her. But Emily was stronger. Heavier. Emily's long auburn hair floated across Bridgett's face.

Bridgett fought her rising panic. She pressed her palm into Emily's face as the two sunk to the bottom of the pool. Suddenly, Emily pulled away from her and swam to the surface. Bridgett pushed her feet against the floor of the pool and followed Emily to the top.

Both women gulped for air after surfacing. Emily's eyes locked with Bridgett's as soon as she had taken a breath. Bridgett reached for the pool's edge. She'd started to pull herself out of the water when she felt Emily's hand on the back of her head.

Emily grabbed a handful of her hair and yanked her back into the pool. Bridgett's hands fell away from the edge as the water came over her face. Before she could react, Emily slammed her forehead into the rounded edge of the pool.

Stunned, Bridgett went limp and sank beneath the water.

As soon as the water rushed over her face, she recovered from the blow and rose to the surface. No sooner had she come up for air when Emily shoved her head into the pool's concrete wall. The world around her spun as Bridgett grabbed weakly for the pool's edge. All the fight within her seemed to slip away as she gripped the side of the pool.

"This is just too easy," she heard Emily say. "I could kill you now if I wanted."

Bridgett didn't have the strength to move. Instead, she clung to the edge of the pool to merely stay afloat.

"But I want you to experience pain before you die. Pain like I've had to live with."

Emily swam next to Bridgett and pulled herself out. Bridgett felt unable to move as she stared straight ahead at Emily's sopping wet boots.

"Stay here. I'll be right back," Emily said.

Bridgett's world was still spinning, and she struggled to hold on to the edge. She leaned her throbbing head against the side of the pool for support.

She's going to get her knife. You have to move, she told herself. But her body wouldn't respond. She didn't have the strength to pull herself out of the water.

Bridgett let her grip fall away from the pool's edge and lay on her back atop the water. She glided her arms through the water as fast and as quietly as her body would allow. Finally, she reached the steps. She climbed out of the pool on her hands and knees. Without standing up, she turned to find Emily.

Emily's back was to her. Her normally curly hair was now pulled straight down her back from the water. She was searching the ground by the palm tree, trying to find her knife. She appeared oblivious that Bridgett had gotten out of the water.

Bridgett crawled a few feet from the pool and grabbed a large garden gnome with both hands. Slowly, she stood to her feet and turned toward Emily. She watched Emily crouch on her hands and knees and reach under a lounge chair. Bridgett closed the distance between them as fast as she could. Her bare feet were silent on the cement.

Emily was beginning to stand when Bridgett slammed the gnome into the back of her head with all her strength. Emily fell to the ground but kept hold of the knife. Bridgett lifted the gnome again with both hands and brought it down a second time atop Emily's head, breaking part of the garden ornament against Emily's forehead. Blood seeped from the cut near Emily's hairline as Bridgett lifted the gnome again.

Emily's arms fell to her sides as she lay against the concrete. She still had a weak grip on the knife. Bridgett stepped on her hand that held the weapon and trembled from the adrenaline pumping through her body.

She didn't want to hit her again. She wasn't a killer. But there was no other way to keep Emily from continuing to attack her.

Bridgett grimaced as she brought the gnome down hard a final time. Emily grunted from the blow and her head fell to the side. Her eyes closed and Bridgett dropped the gnome next to her unmoving form.

Bridgett stepped back and saw that blood was pooling on the top of Emily's scalp, turning her auburn hair crimson at the roots. Bridgett stood watching her, waiting for a sign that Emily was going to recover. But Emily remained still. She was breathing shallowly as blood dripped down the side of her face.

Bridgett ran toward the house. The basement door she'd come through was now closed. She tried the handle, but it was locked. She slammed herself against the door in frustration. The door shook, but it didn't budge.

Bridgett turned and stepped over Emily's body on her way to the pool. She stopped at the water's edge. The pool lights were on and it was easy to see the golf club laying on the bottom. She overcame her repulsion of getting back into the water and dove into the pool. The chlorine stung her eyes as she took a few strokes to get to bottom. She grabbed the club and pushed off the floor of the pool to propel herself to the surface.

She swam awkwardly to the stairs with the club in one hand. Once she was out of the water, she ran back to the house. She jumped over Emily and noticed the pool of blood around her head had grown. When she reached the basement door, Bridgett swung the club at the door's glass panel. It shattered but remained intact after her first swing. It took two more swings before she made a hole in the glass big enough for her to get through.

She stepped through the broken glass and ran for the stairs. She was on the main floor before she noticed the shooting pain in her foot. She lifted her leg and saw a large piece of glass sticking out of her inner sole. Ignoring the pain, she tore the chunk of glass out of her foot and tossed it onto the entryway floor.

"Leo!" she called. "Leo? Baby, where are you?"

"Bridgett?" Paul's voice called from the kitchen.

Thank God.

"Paul!" She ran toward the sound of his voice.

He came out of the kitchen doorway as she was about to go in. They collided and she pressed her hands against his chest.

His look of bewilderment turned to fear as he backed away from her. She was dripping wet from the pool and her palms had left hand prints on his white shirt. His eyes widened. He stepped toward her, gripping her by both shoulders.

"Where's Emily? Is she all right?"

Bridgett started to sob. She shook her head. "No."

"Where is she?" he demanded. "Bridgett, where is Emily? What happened? Where's Leo?" He brought his face within inches of her own. Their noses were nearly touching.

"I-I don't know." Bridgett choked back her tears. "I need your phone. We need to call 911." She sank back against the wall.

"What do you mean you don't know?" he shouted. "Where's my son?"

"Emily—" Bridgett's sobs overtook her voice.

"Emily what?"

Bridgett gripped Paul's arm. "We need to call 911. Chris is dead, and I can't find Leo."

"Who's Chris?"

Bridgett realized Paul would've come in through the garage and hadn't seen her boyfriend lying dead in front of the house.

"Emily ki—"

Paul jerked his head toward a noise at the end of the hall. "Emily!"

CHAPTER FOURTEEN

Bridgett watched in horror as Paul rushed to his wife. Emily leaned against the wall in the entryway. Her head was covered in blood. She looked like she was struggling to stand.

"Oh my—" Paul extended his arms to his wife. "It's gonna be okay, sweetheart. I'm calling 911." He kept a hand on his wife's shoulder as he reached into his pocket for his phone. "What happened? Where's Leo?"

Paul was still pulling out his phone when Bridgett saw Emily's arm tucked behind her back.

"Paul!" Bridgett raced toward him. "It was her!"

He'd halfway turned in the direction of her screams when Emily drew the blade from behind her back and stabbed him in the stomach.

Bridgett came to a standstill a few feet behind him as she watched his eyes grow wide with shock. He stared at his wife. His mouth was open, but no words came out. He placed his hand over hers that gripped the knife she'd plunged into his gut. Emily grit her teeth before shoving the knife farther into her husband's torso.

Fresh tears ran down Bridgett's face as she helplessly

watched him double over in pain before collapsing on the hardwood floor. Emily left the large knife protruding from his abdomen.

Bridgett eyed the glass shard she'd left on the floor, deciding whether to run or fight. Even without her knife, Bridgett wasn't confident she could take the tall woman down. Emily obviously still had plenty of fight left in her.

Emily looked away from her dying husband and locked eyes with Bridgett. Bridgett made her decision. She bolted for the stairs, picking the glass shard off the floor as she went. She took them two at a time, hearing Emily following right behind her. The glass sliced through her palm. When she reached the top, she moved the shard to her other hand, gripping the glass through the fabric of her shirt sleeve as she sprinted to the empty room with the writing on the wall.

She slammed the door closed behind her, but Emily threw it open before she could turn the lock. Bridgett fell to the floor. Emily's bloodied form stepped over her. She grabbed Bridgett by both wrists and dragged her across the plush carpet. Bridgett clutched tight her palm holding the glass.

When they reached the French doors to the balcony, Emily let go of one Bridgett's wrists. Bridgett held on to the glass shard for a better opportunity. All she could reach was Emily's legs, and it would be hard to cut through her thick canvas pants. She kicked and flailed but couldn't break from Emily's firm grip on her wrist.

The French doors swung open. Emily replaced her hand on Bridgett's arm and pulled her fighting form onto the wood deck. Bridgett expected Emily to start beating her on the ground but instead she backed away.

"Get up," Emily said.

Clenching the glass shard in her right hand, Bridgett slowly stood to her feet. Bridgett faced the sister she had never known, her back to the balcony railing. Emily sneered. Bridgett stood still, waiting to defend herself.

Emily charged forward, encircling both hands around Bridgett's neck. Her momentum forced Bridgett backward until her weight pressed against the wrought-iron railing.

She struggled for air as Emily squeezed tighter. Bridgett knew her opportunity had come. She moved the glass past the edge of her bloody fingers.

Bridgett pushed the palm of her left hand against Emily's forehead and forced her head backward. She lifted her right hand and swiped the glass shard through the side of Emily's neck.

Emily cried out and brought her hands to her neck, releasing Bridgett's airway. Emily staggered back. Bridgett pressed her back against the railing and shoved her foot into Emily's chest, knocking her to the ground.

"You bitch!" Bridgett heard her sister say as she climbed on top of the railing. There was no time to think. She looked at the pool three stories below and bent her legs as she prepared to jump. Her feet had almost left the railing when she felt Emily's arms wrap around her lower legs.

Emily yanked both ankles backward. Bridgett's feet slipped off the railing. Her ribs slammed onto the wrought iron.

"Ahh!" She planted her feet on the deck and turned around to face Emily.

Emily was already on the rebound attack. She let out a growl and leapt forward with her hands outstretched at Bridgett's neck. Her long fingers clamped tightly around Bridgett's throat.

Bridgett pressed her palms against Emily's face, trying unsuccessfully to push her away. Emily's hands dug deeper into Bridgett's neck. Bridgett leaned back over the railing in an attempt to move out of Emily's reach. But she couldn't lean far enough. She choked for air as she dug her fingernails into Emily's neck and face. Emily appeared not to even notice.

She heard Emily laugh as her lungs burned for air.

"There's no escape, little sister. You're going to die."

The pressure in her head felt unbearable. Bridgett tried to scream but her vocal cords were squeezed shut. She pressed her back harder into the railing, but she was trapped. There was nowhere to go. And all her strength was rapidly leaving her body.

She thought about Leo as the world around her dimmed. After seeing what she'd done to her husband and to Chris, Bridgett feared Emily was capable of hurting, even killing, her own child.

The panic she had immediately felt was being replaced by a dulling of all her senses. The fight in her subsided as she started to accept that she had already taken her final breath. Everything seemed to slow down. She thought of how sweet Leo looked after she lay him in his crib that night.

It made sense she was his aunt. She had always felt a deeper bond with him than just his nanny. Even though she'd only taken care of him for a month, she loved him.

She tried again to suck in a breath of air. Nothing. Her hands fell away from her sister's face. She prayed Leo would be all right when the balcony railing made a sharp screech. Her body was jolted into the air as the railing gave way. She fell back with Emily on top of her. Emily's hands released her throat as they toppled together over the side.

Bridgett's reflexes took over as she gulped for air. She closed her fingers around a banister rod. Her hand slid until it caught where the rod met the railing. She jerked to a stop as Emily fell past her in a dark blur. Bridgett swung beneath the balcony, suspended by one arm on the railing barely connected to the deck.

She heard the sickening thud of Emily's body smacking against the concrete patio, perfectly timed in a rare moment of silence between the fireworks. Bridgett couldn't bear to look down. The railing let out another loud screech as it strained to hold her weight.

She reached her other arm up to grab the deck, but it was a few inches above her reach. The movement took her mind back to all the hours she'd practiced for her uneven bars routine as a teenager. It was a routine that had won her several medals at regional and national competitions. She'd learned to use the strength in her core to lift her body up and over the bars.

Her uneven bars routines were always her dad's favorite. He was proud of all her gymnastic accomplishments, but her skills on the uneven bars had seemed to impress him the most. She had a clear memory of him in the crowd at one of her toughest competitions. Standing. Cheering. Applauding.

Bridgett pumped her legs back and forth, using her abdominal muscles to gain enough momentum to grab hold of the balcony. Her fingers had barely grasped onto the wood ledge when the wrought iron railing gave way. Pain soared through her left hand as she gripped the edge of the deck with all her might.

The railing clamored to the patio below as Bridgett struggled to maintain her grip on the deck. She grabbed the edge of the balcony with her other hand and swung her foot over the side. She hooked her ankle around the railing post still attached to the deck.

Her left hand slipped from the blood that covered her palm. Using every last bit of strength she had, she let go of the deck with her bloodied hand and reached for the post across from the one that held her ankle. She pushed against the edge of the deck with her right hand and rotated her body onto the balcony. She rolled away from the edge before coming to a stop.

Tears streamed down the sides of her face as she looked at the colorful fireworks booming in the night sky. She crawled to the edge and peered below.

Emily's unmoving, crumpled form lay face-up on the patio. Her eyes were open, staring into nothing. The piece of railing that had fallen lay next to her body on the concrete. Bridgett wiped the tears from her eyes and backed into the house.

Once inside, she ran downstairs.

"Paul!"

Paul lay in the same spot where he'd collapsed after Emily stabbed him. The large knife still protruded from his abdomen. A puddle of blood had formed around the blade on his white shirt. Bridgett knelt at his side. His face was nearly as white as his hair.

Please, God. Don't let him die, too.

His eyelids were barely open. Bridgett felt the side of his Adam's apple for a pulse when she saw a shallow rise and fall of his chest.

"Paul!" She gently shook his shoulders.

His eyelids fluttered open.

"Thank God!" she cried. "You're alive."

"Where's Leo?" he whispered.

She shook her head. "I don't know. I need to call 911. Where's your phone?"

He lifted his blood-covered hand holding his iPhone. "I already called. They're on their way."

"Okay. Good."

Bridgett wondered if she should put something on his wound to try and stop the bleeding. But she worried she might do further damage if she inadvertently dislodged the knife by applying pressure around it. She prayed the medics would get there soon. She looked around for something to put under his head.

"I'll be right back, Paul."

She ran to the living room and grabbed a pillow off the couch. She was halfway down the hall to the entryway when she heard the sound of Leo's cry.

CHAPTER FIFTEEN

Bridgett stopped at the door to Paul's home office. He was alive! She threw open the door. Leo squinted from the light shining in from the hall as she entered the dark room. He stood in his pajamas with his hands on the side of a playpen.

"Leo!"

She heard sirens in the distance. She scooped the boy up in her arms and pulled him tightly against her chest. Tears ran down her face.

"You're okay." She laughed through her tears as the boy patted her arm.

"Bridg-ee."

Her heart melted at the sound of his sweet voice. The sirens grew louder, then flashing lights filled the office window.

Her foot stepped on something small and hard as she moved toward the office door. She recognized it immediately. Holding Leo firmly in her arms, she knelt and picked her phone up off the floor.

She took the boy into the hall and yelled in Paul's direction. "I found Leo! He's okay!"

She walked closer to the entryway as four uniformed

police entered the home. Their guns were drawn but aimed at the floor. Bridgett stayed back, not wanting Leo to see his father that way.

A female police officer approached her, stopping a few feet from her.

"Ma'am, Officer Timmons is going to take the child from you and make sure he's okay."

Bridgett watched a male officer holster his weapon and take slow steps toward her. The female officer kept her gun pointed at the floor. Bridgett noticed her finger wasn't on the trigger, but out straight against the gun barrel.

"When he takes the child, I want you to place your hands on top of your head. Understand?" the female officer said.

Bridgett nodded. "Yes."

She let the male officer take Leo from her arms, although she hated to let him go so soon after finding him.

"It's okay." Bridgett smiled at the boy to reassure him as Officer Timmons carried him out of the house.

Bridgett did as she was told and placed her hands on her head. The female officer came behind her and cuffed Bridgett's hands behind her back.

Another officer knelt next to Paul and lifted his radio to his mouth. "Tell the medics it's safe for them to come in."

"Are you the child's mother?" the female officer asked.

"No, I'm his nanny."

"Is he the boy's father?" She pointed to Paul.

"Yes."

"Do you know who stabbed him?"

"His wife. Emily."

"And is she still in the home?"

"Umm...no, she's outside. In the backyard by the pool. I think she's dead."

"I'm going to take you outside where I'll ask you some more questions, okay?"

Bridgett heard more sirens approaching as they stepped outside. Seconds later, an ambulance pulled into the drive. The officer led Bridgett away from the house.

Bridgett craned her neck as they walked by Chris's truck. She wanted to see him again. Wanted it to not be real. She wished for a sign that it wasn't too late to save him. But the medics rushed past his body as they pushed a stretcher into the house for Paul, confirming what she already knew to be true.

The officer led Bridgett around the side of the garage to a small courtyard, blocking her view of the activity in the driveway. The courtyard was illuminated by tall, decorative lamp posts.

"I see you've got a bad cut on your back. Another ambulance will be arriving soon. We'll have you checked out when they arrive. Is there anyone else still in the home?" the officer asked.

"No. My boyfriend. Chris. He's in the driveway. He's——" her voice broke.

"We found him."

Bridgett felt the officer's hand on her shoulder.

"Can you tell me what happened tonight?"

Bridgett was halfway through recounting the events of the night when she heard another ambulance arrive. She'd already heard the siren of the first ambulance when it left to take Paul to the hospital.

"And then what happened?" the officer asked her.

Bridgett went back to explaining all that had happened that night. Less than ten minutes later, she heard the ambulance's siren as it pulled out of the Coopers' drive. She paused from her story and turned her head toward the driveway, even though the garage still blocked her view. She had thought the ambulance came for her, since they'd already taken Paul.

Maybe they'd taken Leo to make certain he didn't have any injuries. Because Emily was dead. Right?

CHAPTER SIXTEEN

"Oh, no," Tess said, seeing the patrol car parked in front of Paul and Emily's front gate.

"Maybe Paul called the police as a precaution." But Blake had a bad feeling as he slowed the car at the Coopers' front entrance.

The gate was open, but an officer stood in its place. He approached Blake's unmarked Ford. Blake rolled down his window. He didn't recognize the officer. He pulled out his badge and ID.

"Seattle Homicide," Blake said.

"Wow, you guys got here fast."

Blake heard Tess draw in a sharp breath. "We're actually looking for her brother." Blake motioned toward Tess. "He was working here tonight, and we haven't been able to get a hold of him."

"Oh." The officer looked confused.

"There's been a homicide?" Blake asked.

His phone rang before the officer could answer. He recognized the number when he lifted his phone. It was the Chief Dispatcher. Blake put the phone to his ear.

"Detective Stephenson."

Tess leaned over to listen in on the call.

"Hey, Detective. There's been a homicide. Twenty-three-year-old male. It appears his throat was slit. Massive amounts of blood loss."

Blake looked at his girlfriend as the dispatcher gave him Paul and Emily's address. Her eyes were wide with shock.

"I'm already there," Blake said.

Tess unbuckled her seatbelt and threw open the passenger door.

"Tess! Wait!"

Blake threw his phone onto his empty passenger seat as Tess bolted through the open gate. The patrol officer swore and got on his radio. Blake jumped out of the car and chased after Tess.

She was already halfway down the long driveway. The wail of an ambulance siren muted her scream as she neared Chris's landscape truck. Blake ran onto the front lawn to move out of the emergency vehicle's path.

He watched two officers fight to restrain Tess. She was within about ten feet of Chris's truck. Blake saw why Tess was fighting so hard to get past them. Chris's body lay on the drive behind his vehicle. His taillights cast a soft red glow over his still form and the large pool of blood that surrounded his body. Placards with blue flashing lights marked a perimeter around the blood.

"Chris!" Tess screamed as the officers forced her onto her knees.

Blake held out his badge as he ran toward the officers. "Seattle Homicide. He's her brother. I'm sorry. I'll take her away."

The officers looked at his badge as one prepared to cuff her. Tess's screams had turned into a violent cry. She stopped fighting the officers as Blake knelt next to her and encased her in his arms. She let her body fall against his, shaking as she wept for her brother.

Blake fought back his own tears as the two officers cautiously released Tess into his hold. Tess allowed Blake to help her stand to her feet.

"Come on," he said. "Let me take you home."

She didn't budge from where she stood.

"You can't be here, Tess. This isn't your case. He's your brother, it's a conflict of interest."

She looked at Chris's body before reluctantly allowing Blake to lead her back to his car.

"I'm sorry," Blake said to the officer still at the gate.

"It's okay," he said, seeing the distraught look on Tess's face.

Tess turned to Blake as he tried to help her get into his car. "Who would do that to him?"

"I don't know, but I'm sure they'll find out."

"Won't you find out? Isn't this your case?"

"I don't see how I can take it. You're my girlfriend. He's your brother. A defense attorney could use that to rip apart the case. Adams can take it. He'll be here soon. We can wait in the car and I'll talk to him when he gets here."

"Okay."

"I'm so sorry, Tess." He wrapped her tightly in his arms.

She sobbed quietly against his chest before slowly climbing into his passenger seat.

CHAPTER SEVENTEEN

By the time the next ambulance got there, Bridgett had told her everything. The officer uncuffed her.

"Where's Leo?" Bridgett asked the officer as the team of medics got out of the ambulance.

"He's safe. Don't worry. We'll make sure he's well taken care of until we get this all sorted out."

A young medic led Bridgett to the back of the ambulance where she sat for him to take her vital signs and assess her injuries.

A few minutes later, an unmarked car pulled up behind the ambulance and Bridgett watched a muscular, middle-aged man climb out of the driver's side. Unlike everyone else who'd responded to the scene until now, he wasn't wearing a uniform. His light gray suit fit him well. He walked across the driveway to speak with a couple of the first-responding officers.

"You get hit in the head tonight?" The medic shone a pen light in one of her eyes and then the other.

She told him how Emily had slammed her head against the side of the pool.

"I think you may have a concussion." He moved to look

at the knife wound on her back. "That's a pretty deep cut," he said. "You're going to need some stitches. It's still bleeding in some areas. I'm going to put a bandage on that before we go."

The man in the gray suit appeared behind the open doors at the rear of the ambulance. He extended his hand to Bridgett.

"I'm Detective Adams, but you can call me Kyle," he said as she accepted his handshake.

"Bridgett," she said.

"I've spoken to Officer Crawford. Sounds like you've had quite a rough night."

"Yes."

"Paul was coherent enough before they took him to Harborview to corroborate your statement that his wife was the one who stabbed him. I know you've already spoken to Officer Crawford, but can you tell me again what happened tonight?"

She told him everything she'd told the officer, starting from when she'd made Chris leave. Something she wished now she could take back. She ended with telling him how Emily had planned to make her look guilty of Chris's death and stealing the necklace.

He crossed his arms after she finished her story. "So, your dad, who called you earlier tonight, is also Emily's dad? But you never knew about her?"

"That's what she said, yes. And Emily had a picture of my father with her mother and her when she was three years old. But, no, I never knew about her."

"We need to get her to the hospital," the medic told the detective after he'd finished applying her bandages. "You can lean back against the stretcher now," he said to Bridgett.

"Here's my card in case you remember anything else."

Bridgett took the business card Adams held out toward her.

"As long as the evidence matches up with your statement, you don't have anything to worry about. I'll find out the truth."

She felt reassured looking into his eyes. There was something about him that made her feel she could trust him.

"Is Emily—" She couldn't bring herself to say the word.

"No. She sustained some serious injuries, but she still had a pulse when the medics arrived. We'll have to wait to find out the extent of her injuries from her fall and those blows to her head."

A sense of heaviness came over her, and then she felt guilty for wishing Leo's mother was dead.

"I might come by the hospital once you've been treated and take you to Police Headquarters for an interview, if you're well enough."

"Okay," she said before the medic closed the rear ambulance doors.

As the ambulance pulled out of the home's long private drive, she promised herself she would always find a way to be a part of Leo's life. They needed each other.

Bridgett's phone rang in her front pocket. She pulled it out and stared at the name that lit up the screen. Dad.

"You can answer that if you want," the medic said.

She let it ring for a second longer before using her thumb to press Ignore. She didn't know what to say to the man she thought she knew.

EPILOGUE

Four Months Later

Tess looked across the courtroom, thinking Emily had no right to look as dignified as she did. She looked calm, despite being on trial for Chris's murder. She sat in a wheelchair next to her defense attorney, her hands folded in her lap. Her auburn hair was pulled back into a sophisticated bun at the nape of her neck.

The fall from her third-story balcony had left her unable to walk. Tess feared her disability would be a cause for sympathy from the jury. Emily had added to her unconscionable actions by pleading not guilty by reason of insanity. Tess could only hope the jury would be smart enough to see through her defense.

It was only the first week of the trial, and Tess was ready for it to be over. Although she desperately wanted justice for her younger brother, it was agonizing having to relive the night he died by sitting through the trial.

Nathan and Chloe sat to her right and Adams to her left. Since Adams was the lead investigator in Chris's murder, he was obligated to be present at the trial. But Tess had to take vacation time in order to be there.

Tess forced herself to look away from Emily, wishing Blake could've been there with her. He'd wanted to, but he wasn't able to get the time off work. She'd attended a few trials in the ten months she'd been a homicide detective but being present at Chris's trial was more painful than she had even imagined. She now had a deeper understanding of what victims' family members went through. She felt her eyes brim with tears, and she worked to blink them away.

The prosecuting attorney stood from his chair. "The State would like to call its first witness, Bridgett Hammond, to the stand."

Tess turned her head to the end of her row. Her eyes followed Chris's girlfriend, who had been sitting between Paul and an older couple, as she walked to the witness stand.

After swearing to tell the truth, Bridgett straightened the hem of her pencil skirt and stepped into the witness box. She locked eyes with her father as the prosecutor moved toward her. She hadn't spoken to him for weeks after that horrible night and still hadn't forgiven him.

When Bridgett finally confronted him about being Emily's father, he'd been shocked to learn of Emily's confession before admitting to having another child. Although his recollection was different from what Emily had told her. He claimed to have met Bridgett's mom right after his divorce from Emily's mother. Not long after getting full custody of Emily, her mother had moved across the country.

Bridgett recalled her father's tear-streaked face as he told his side of the story months earlier, sitting across his kitchen table from her.

"For years, I called and sent letters, but they were never returned. Not long after we had you, my letters were returned to sender. Their phone number was disconnected, and I had no forwarding address." A sob escaped her father's throat as he looked down at his hands. "I know I should've tried harder, and there's no excuse for that. Your mother and I were so happy...and I accepted that Emily's mom wanted no part of me in her life." After a moment of silence, he continued. "I didn't learn that she'd died until nearly ten years later. And I didn't know Emily was in the foster system." A tear dripped off the side of his face onto the table. "I should've tried harder to find her. I never forgot her, and I'm so sorry for not telling you."

"And mom knew?" Bridgett's voice came out quiet.

He nodded. "We planned on telling you one day but..." His voice trailed off.

"But what?" she asked. What excuse could there be for not telling her she had a sister?

Bridgett forced her mind back to the present. Her father gave her a reassuring nod before she cut a glance at her older half-sister—Chris's killer—who stared at her from her wheelchair behind the defense table.

The prosecutor cleared his throat. "Can you describe your relationship to Paul and Emily Cooper for the court?"

Bridgett braced herself to recount the worst night of her life. She turned away from Emily to face the jury. "I was their summer nanny."

Tess assessed the jury's impression of the young nanny for the duration of Bridgett's testimony. Bridgett held her composure throughout the defense attorney's cross examination, and Tess could see why Chris liked her. Not only was she beautiful and smart, but her love for Chris was evident.

Tess swallowed as a lump formed in her throat. *What a life they could've had.*

When Bridgett stepped out of the witness box, Tess felt herself relax. She returned to her seat and Tess squeezed her older brother's hand. For the first time that week, Tess was confident the truth would prevail.

WANT MORE?

Get your FREE bonus content and
deleted scenes at
AUDREYJCOLE.COM/sign-up

DETECTIVES BLAKE STEPHENSON
AND TESS RICHARDS TEAM UP WITH
SERGEANT WADE McKINNON IN
THE NEXT EMERALD CITY THRILLER

MALORIE'S BEST FRIEND IS MISSING. BUT
DUE TO HER FRIEND'S WILD PAST, NO
ONE IS WORRIED—UNTIL ANOTHER MED
STUDENT'S PARTIAL REMAINS WASH
ASHORE A SEATTLE BEACH...

ALSO BY AUDREY J. COLE

EMERALD CITY THRILLERS

THE RECIPIENT

INSPIRED BY MURDER

THE SUMMER NANNY

VIABLE HOSTAGE

STANDALONES

THE PILOT'S DAUGHTER

THE FINAL HUNT (JUNE 2022)

PREVIEW OF
VIABLE HOSTAGE

CHAPTER ONE

The purr of the yacht's idling engines was the only noise on the calm midnight water of Puget Sound. Until the garbage bag filled with Gretchen's chopped-up body splashed into the sea.

The man returned to the helm of the fifty-foot motor cruiser. He thrust the throttles forward. The vessel vibrated under his feet as the five-hundred-horsepower dual engines roared to life. He cruised forward before making a wide turn back to the city, careful not to run over the bag full of Gretchen's remains as they sank to the bottom.

He had two more bags to dump but thought it best not to sink them all in the same spot.

He sped past the southern tip of Bainbridge Island and veered right toward Elliott Bay. There were faint lights in the distance from the large waterfront estates that bordered the densely wooded island. It would've been a tranquil scene if it weren't for Gretchen's dismembered corpse that filled the remaining trash bags on board.

When his depth finder reached five hundred feet, he

threw the boat into neutral. He hurried to the stern where two large black garbage bags rested against the side of the vessel.

He grimaced slightly as he lifted the heavy bag over the edge. Another splash. He looked over the side and waited a moment for it to sink before returning to the helm.

It wasn't Gretchen's death that bothered him. He couldn't believe it had gone so wrong. After all that planning. All that work. For *nothing*.

Gretchen had been the perfect subject. No one even missed her after she disappeared. He'd already been making plans for this kind of research before he'd learned of Gretchen's unwanted pregnancy from a one-night stand.

He had everything in place by the time her fetus got close to viability. Gretchen's kidnapping had gone to a T. His research was about to begin. Until he screwed everything up.

He slammed the throttles into full speed. When he reached the north end of Bainbridge, he eased up on the power. The yacht idled halfway between the island and downtown Seattle before he killed the engines. He moved to the back of the boat. Looking at the dark water that surrounded him, he thought of the two bags containing Gretchen's remains already lying on the floor of the Sound.

He lifted the remaining bag and swung it over the side. He stared at the water's surface as his last three months of work and planning sank to the bottom. A ferry horn blared into the midnight silence, and he jumped at the sound.

He cocked his head and saw that he had drifted into the direct path of the Bainbridge ferry. The large vessel looked less than a hundred feet away. The ferry lights nearly blinded him.

The ferry sounded its second warning, which muted the string of expletives that came out of the man's mouth. He ran to the helm and pushed the throttles forward. Nothing happened. The man swore, remembering he'd turned off the engines. He pressed the ignition starter, but the yacht remained quiet.

The ferry blared its horn another time, now less than fifty feet away. The man spun around to see the ferry cutting to the left to move out of his path. The man pulled the throttles back to neutral and pushed the starter again. The engines hummed. The man shoved the throttles forward. He sped away, nearly clipping the ferry's starboard side as it sounded its horn a final time.

The man slammed his fist against the side of the boat. The whole point of dumping the body at midnight was to avoid being seen. Good thing he'd weighted down the bags.

His heart gradually stopped racing as he cruised toward the Ballard Locks just north of the city that would lead him back to Lake Union. He looked around at the Sound's calm waters, thinking of Gretchen's remains down there.

There was only one thing left to do. He'd have to find another pregnant woman that no one would miss. And start over.

ABOUT THE AUTHOR

Audrey J. Cole is a registered nurse and a writer of thrillers set in Seattle. After living in Australia for the last five years, Audrey has returned to the Pacific Northwest where she resides with her husband and two children.

Connect with Audrey:

f facebook.com/AudreyJCole

BB bookbub.com/authors/Audrey-J-Cole

instagram.com/AudreyJCole/

You can also visit her website:
www.AUDREYJCOLE.com

Made in the USA
Middletown, DE
27 December 2022

20490891R00061